Country File
The Caribbean

Ian Graham

A⁺

Smart Apple Media

First published in 2001 by Franklin Watts
96 Leonard Street, London EC2A 4XD, UK

Franklin Watts Australia
56 O'Riordan Street, Alexandria, NSW 2015

Country File: The Caribbean produced for Franklin Watts by
Bender Richardson White, PO Box 266, Uxbridge, UK.

Project Editor: Lionel Bender, Text Editor: Peter
Harrison, Designer: Ben White, Picture Researcher:
Cathy Stastny, Media Conversion and Make-up:
Mike Pilley/Radius, Production: Kim Richardson
Graphics: Mike Pilley/Radius, Maps: Stefan Chabluk
Copyright © 2001 Bender Richardson White

For Franklin Watts, Series Editor: Adrian Cole, Art
Director: Jonathan Hair

Published in the United States by Smart Apple Media
1980 Lookout Drive, North Mankato, MN 56003

Library of Congress Cataloging-in-Publication Data

Graham, Ian, 1953–
The Caribbean / by Ian Graham.
p. cm. — (Country files)
Includes index.
Summary: Describes the geography, economy,
government, people, transportation, education, and
culture of the Caribbean Area.
ISBN 1-58340-205-5
1. Caribbean Area—Juvenile literature.
[1. Caribbean Area.] I. Title.

F2161.5 .G73 2002
972.9—dc21   2002017028

9 8 7 6 5 4 3 2 1

The Author
Ian Graham is a full-time writer and
editor of nonfiction books. He has
written more than 100 books for
children.

Contents

Welcome to the Caribbean 4

The Land 6

The People 8

Urban and Rural Life 10

Farming and Fishing 12

Resources and Industry 14

Transportation 16

Education 18

Sports and Leisure 20

Daily Life and Religion 22

The Arts and Media 24

Government 26

Place in the World 28

Database 30

Glossary 31

Index 32

Welcome to the Caribbean

The Caribbean, or West Indies, is known to most people for its blue skies, white beaches, tropical palms, and crystal-clear sea. It is an area of many islands with different cultures and traditions.

The region includes the Caribbean Sea and the island chain that separates it from the Atlantic Ocean. The chain stretches 1,990 miles (3,200 km).

Island chains

The islands fall into three main archipelagos: the Greater Antilles, Lesser Antilles, and the Bahamas. Trinidad & Tobago and Barbados lie to the south and east of the Lesser Antilles but are not considered to be part of them.

The Greater Antilles consists of the four largest Caribbean islands: Cuba, Hispaniola (shared by Haiti and the Dominican Republic), Jamaica, and Puerto Rico.

This book concentrates on the islands that were former British colonies: Jamaica, Barbados, the Bahamas, Trinidad & Tobago, and most of the smaller islands of the Lesser Antilles.

The fishing port of Soufrière on St. Lucia, one of the Windward Islands. Surrounded by palms, Soufrière is the island's main center of coconut production. ▼

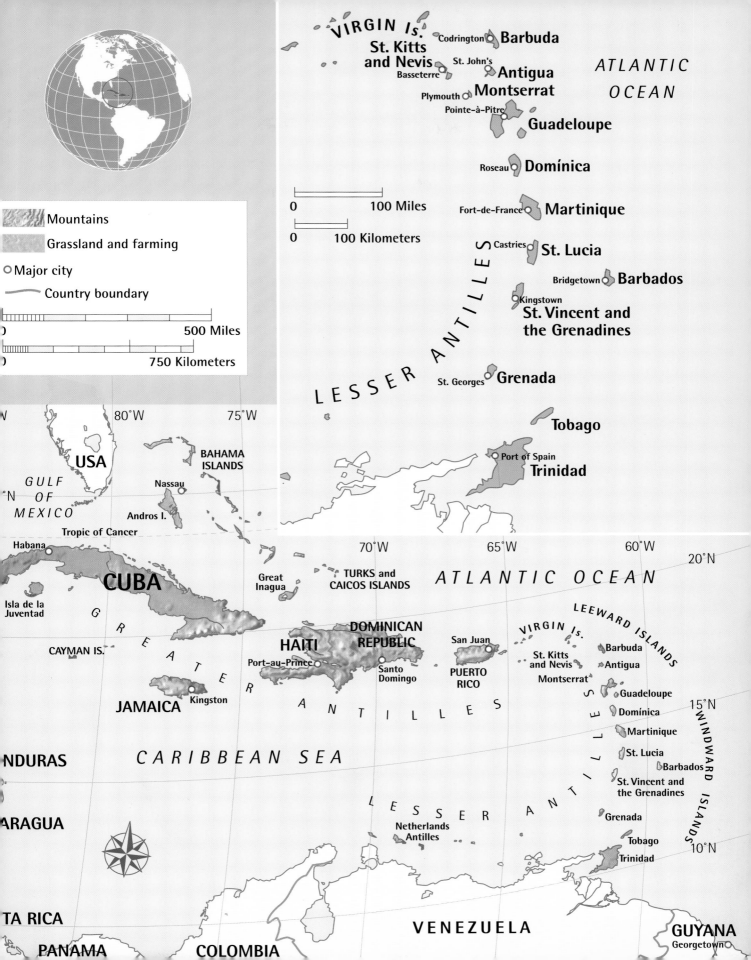

VIRGIN Is.
Codrington ● **Barbuda**
St. Kitts and Nevis
St. John's
Basseterre ● **Antigua**
Montserrat
Plymouth ●
Pointe-à-Pitre ●
Guadeloupe

ATLANTIC OCEAN

Roseau ● **Domínica**

Fort-de-France ● **Martinique**

Castries ● **St. Lucia**

Bridgetown ● **Barbados**

Kingstown ●
St. Vincent and the Grenadines

LESSER ANTILLES

St. Georges ● **Grenada**

Tobago

Port of Spain ●
Trinidad

| 0 | 100 Miles |
| 0 | 100 Kilometers |

Mountains

Grassland and farming

○ **Major city**

Country boundary

| 0 | | | 500 Miles |
| 0 | | | 750 Kilometers |

80°W   75°W

USA

GULF OF MEXICO

BAHAMA ISLANDS

Nassau ●

Andros I.

Tropic of Cancer

Habana ●

CUBA

Isla de la Juventad

CAYMAN IS.

Great Inagua

TURKS and CAICOS ISLANDS

G R E A T E R   A N T I L L E S

HAITI
Port-au-Prince ●

DOMINICAN REPUBLIC
Santo Domingo ●

San Juan ●
PUERTO RICO

ATLANTIC OCEAN   20°N

VIRGIN Is.
St. Kitts and Nevis
Montserrat

LEEWARD ISLANDS

Barbuda
Antigua

JAMAICA
Kingston ●

Guadeloupe
Domínica   15°N

WINDWARD ISLANDS

Martinique
St. Lucia
Barbados
St. Vincent and the Grenadines

C A R I B B E A N   S E A

Grenada

Tobago   10°N
Trinidad

L E S S E R   A N T I L L E S

NDURAS

ARAGUA

Netherlands Antilles

70°W   65°W   60°W

TA RICA

PANAMA   **COLOMBIA**   **VENEZUELA**   **GUYANA**
Georgetown

The Land

The steady, warm temperatures of the Caribbean islands can be accompanied by heavy rain. All year round, daytime temperatures are 77 to 86 °F (25 to 30 °C) at sea level, or slightly cooler in the mountains. At night, it rarely falls below 59 °F (15 °C).

Moist air blowing in from the Atlantic Ocean makes some of the islands very humid, especially between June and November (the wet season). Some of the Leeward Islands receive as much as 35 inches (8,890 mm) of rain each year, while the islands closest to the South American coast may receive as little as one inch (250 mm). Violent tropical storms and hurricanes can strike any time between July and October, although the southernmost islands are usually spared the devastating effects.

Volcanic islands

The Caribbean islands vary widely in size. The Bahamas have a total area of 5,382 square miles (13,940 sq km), for example, while Anguilla is only 35 square miles (91 sq km). The largest islands are the most mountainous.

Many of the islands have active or dormant volcanoes such as the twin peaks of the Pitons, a familiar landmark on St. Lucia in the Windward Islands. One of the most active volcanoes in the region is Mount Soufrière on St. Vincent, a former British colony at the southern end of the Windward Islands. Mount Soufrière erupted in 1812, 1902, 1971, and 1979, when most of the island had to be evacuated.

Animal Life

Lizards and snakes are found on all the Caribbean islands, but only Trinidad has a variety of mammals, including monkeys and sloths. The most colorful creatures are the birds, especially parrots and hummingbirds. The sea teems with life, too. Coral reefs along the islands' eastern coasts are home to more than 1,000 species of fish.

Periodic rainfall maintains the lush vegetation on the island of St. Vincent. St. Vincent's plant life includes coconut palms, hibiscus, and poinsettia. ▼

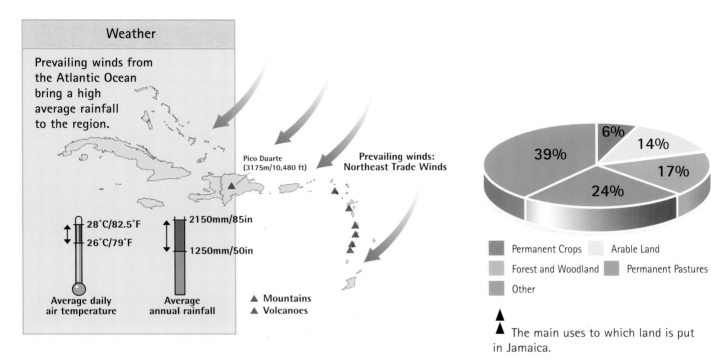

Weather

Prevailing winds from the Atlantic Ocean bring a high average rainfall to the region.

Pico Duarte
(3175m/10,480 ft)

Prevailing winds:
Northeast Trade Winds

28°C/82.5°F
26°C/79°F

2150mm/85in
1250mm/50in

Average daily
air temperature

Average
annual rainfall

▲ Mountains
▲ Volcanoes

6% 14%
17%
24%
39%

■ Permanent Crops □ Arable Land
■ Forest and Woodland ■ Permanent Pastures
■ Other

▲
▲ The main uses to which land is put in Jamaica.

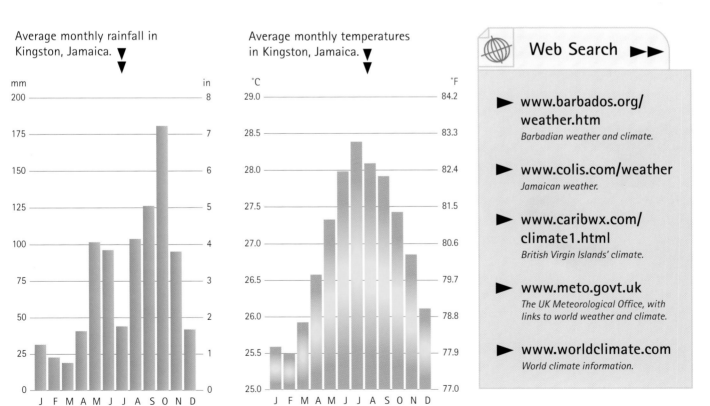

Average monthly rainfall in Kingston, Jamaica. ▼▼

Average monthly temperatures in Kingston, Jamaica. ▼▼

Web Search ►►

► www.barbados.org/
   weather.htm
   Barbadian weather and climate.

► www.colis.com/weather
   Jamaican weather.

► www.caribwx.com/
   climate1.html
   British Virgin Islands' climate.

► www.meto.govt.uk
   The UK Meteorological Office, with links to world weather and climate.

► www.worldclimate.com
   World climate information.

The People

As a result of the area's stormy history of invasion and slavery, the Caribbean is populated by people from many different ethnic backgrounds. Few of the Caribbean's original inhabitants remain. The many different languages spoken reflect the wide range of places from which Caribbean people's ancestors came.

Most of the 36 million people who live in the Caribbean today are descended from those brought from West Africa in the 16th and 17th centuries to work as slaves on sugar plantations. The native Caribbean people were almost completely wiped out by European invaders.

 Origins

The Caribbean is named after the Carib Indians. They lived in the Lesser Antilles when the first Spanish explorers arrived in the 15th century. The warlike Caribs had driven out the islands' original inhabitants, the Arawak Indians.

People from many different ethnic backgrounds mingle at a street market on Curaçao, in the Lesser Antilles. The first inhabitants of the Caribbean were Arawak Indians. ▼

Many languages

A wide range of languages are spoken in the Caribbean today. Many people still speak the languages of the European countries that colonized the islands, including Spanish, English, French, and Dutch. Slaves developed their own versions of these languages, called pidgin and creole.

A second wave of people arrived in the 19th century and brought new languages such as Hindi, Urdu, and Chinese. Immigrants from India and their descendants became known as East Indians to distinguish them from the existing Caribbean people, or West Indians.

One language from six

Some of the Caribbean languages spoken today are combinations of as many as six other languages. Papiemento is spoken in Aruba and the Netherlands Antilles. It includes words taken from Spanish, Portuguese, English, Dutch, and African languages, as well as from the local native language.

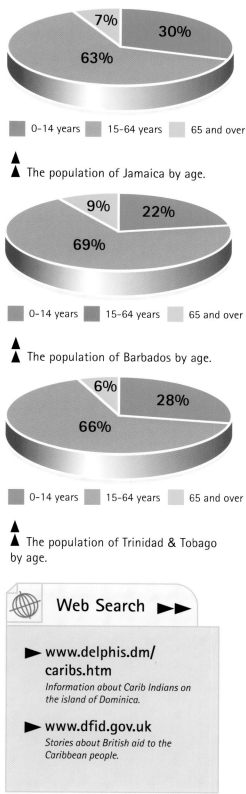

▲ The population of Jamaica by age.

▲ The population of Barbados by age.

▲ The population of Trinidad & Tobago by age.

Web Search ▶▶

▶ www.delphis.dm/caribs.htm
Information about Carib Indians on the island of Dominica.

▶ www.dfid.gov.uk
Stories about British aid to the Caribbean people.

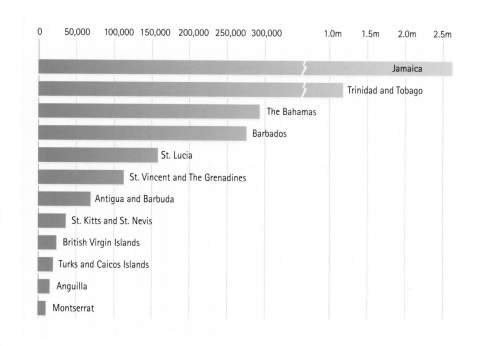

▲ Population figures for some of the islands in the Caribbean.

Urban and Rural Life

Before the rapid growth in tourism and trade, most of the region's people worked in agriculture. Now, more than half the population lives in urban areas. Fewer people live in rural villages and work the land.

Towns and cities throughout the Caribbean grew dramatically during the last century. More and more people left the countryside, hoping to find better jobs and more comfortable living conditions in urban areas. Despite this, Caribbean cities remain relatively small. Only a handful have populations of more than a million people.

A few of the largest cities have busy, multi-lane roads lined with high-rise office blocks, but most are less developed. The region's picturesque coastal towns are popular with tourists. Yachts line the modern marinas and cruise liners dock at the quays. Grand buildings and imposing monuments from the colonial era still stand in many places, giving the towns an historic flavor.

 Kingston, Jamaica

Over half a million people live in the Jamaican capital, Kingston, and about 200,000 more in the surrounding suburbs.

Kingston was founded in 1692 and built to a neat grid system. Its name means "king's town" and honors the British king, William III.

Jamaica became a British colony in 1655. At Port Royal, 17th-century cannons still point out to sea. They were there to defend the island against Dutch, Spanish, or French attack.

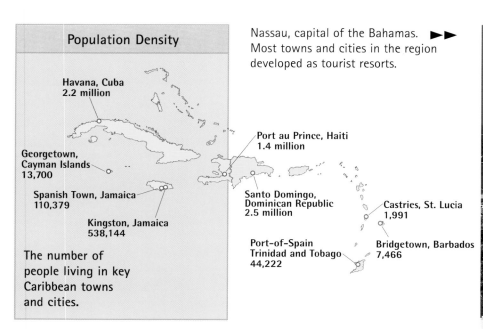

Population Density

Havana, Cuba
2.2 million

Georgetown, Cayman Islands
13,700

Spanish Town, Jamaica
110,379

Kingston, Jamaica
538,144

Port au Prince, Haiti
1.4 million

Santo Domingo, Dominican Republic
2.5 million

Castries, St. Lucia
1,991

Port-of-Spain Trinidad and Tobago
44,222

Bridgetown, Barbados
7,466

The number of people living in key Caribbean towns and cities.

Nassau, capital of the Bahamas. ►► Most towns and cities in the region developed as tourist resorts.

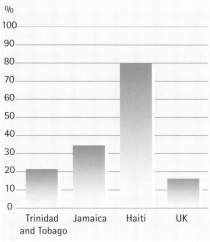

◄◄ A wooden shanty at Sandy Bay in Jamaica. More than a third of Jamaicans live in poverty, mostly on the outskirts of large towns and cities.

▲ The percentage of people living in poverty, compared to the United Kingdom. In the US, it is 11.3%.

◄◄ Percentage of people working in agriculture.

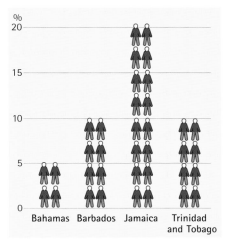

Street Markets

People from urban and rural areas meet at the many fruit and vegetable markets. Country people bring surplus produce from their plots into the towns to be sold. The food on sale includes root vegetables, such as yams and eddoes, as well as plantains, bananas, and squashes.

In cities and countryside

Most of the poorest people in the Caribbean live on the outskirts of the cities, in small wooden houses that they have built themselves. Often these shacks or shanties do not even have a supply of electricity or any clean, piped water.

In the countryside people make a living by working on plantations, or they grow their own food on small plots of land.

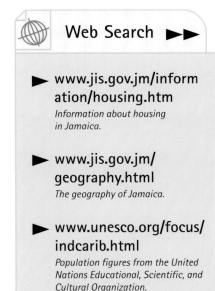

Web Search ►►

► www.jis.gov.jm/inform ation/housing.htm
Information about housing in Jamaica.

► www.jis.gov.jm/ geography.html
The geography of Jamaica.

► www.unesco.org/focus/ indcarib.html
Population figures from the United Nations Educational, Scientific, and Cultural Organization.

Farming and Fishing

The Caribbean's warm, wet climate is excellent for growing sugar cane, coffee, and bananas. Unfortunately, there is always the risk of violent storms that can destroy a valuable crop in minutes.

Good farming land is rare in the Caribbean, so most of the islands need to import food. The smallest islands, such as the Caymans and the Turks & Caicos, rely on imports for almost all of their food.

Principal crops

The most important crops are sugar cane, bananas, coffee beans, cocoa, and tobacco. Arrowroot is an important export for the island of St. Vincent. Crops are grown on estates or plantations, the largest covering 600 acres (250 h) or more, and exported all over the world.

In contrast to these large plantations, people who live in the countryside grow food on their own small plots of land, which are rarely larger than eight acres (3 h). On the smaller islands this is the only form of agriculture. The people keep a few hens, pigs, goats, and in some cases a cow for milk. They grow traditional crops of sweet potatoes, plantains, yams, and cassava.

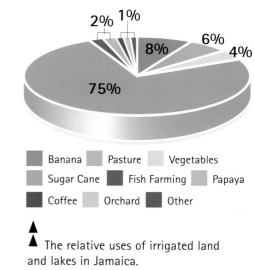

2% 1% 8% 6% 4%
75%

- Banana
- Sugar Cane
- Coffee
- Pasture
- Fish Farming
- Orchard
- Vegetables
- Papaya
- Other

▲ The relative uses of irrigated land and lakes in Jamaica.

Sugar-Making

1. The sugar cane stalks are crushed for their sugary sap.
2. The cloudy sap is left in tanks to clear. Any solid particles sink to the bottom.
3. The clear sap is boiled to make a syrup.
4. The concentrated syrup is dried to produce brown sugar.
5. Refining and purifying this makes white sugar.

◄◄ A banana plantation on St. Lucia. The island produces over 77,000 tons (70,000 t) of bananas each year.

12

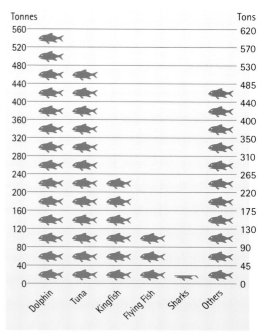

▲ Yearly fishing catches by boats
▲ from St. Lucia.

▲
▲ A fisherman off Grenada holds a
puffer fish that was trapped in his net.
This fish will be returned to the sea.

Food from the sea

The sea around the Caribbean islands is rich in fish, but most are small reef fish that cannot be caught in large enough numbers for commercial profit. Only a few fishing grounds are suitable for large-scale fishing, so most of the fish eaten in the region is imported.

Farming and Fishing

The only large-scale fishing occurs around the Bahamas.

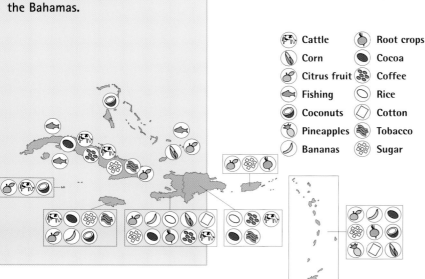

Cattle   Root crops
Corn   Cocoa
Citrus fruit   Coffee
Fishing   Rice
Coconuts Cotton
Pineapples Tobacco
Bananas   Sugar

Web Search ▶▶

▶ **www.cbea.org**
Website of the Caribbean Banana Exporters Association.

▶ **www.jamaicancoffee. gov.jm**
About Jamaica's coffee industry.

▶ **www.caricom–fisheries. com**
Fishing industry profiles for all CARICOM countries.

Resources and Industry

The Caribbean attracts visitors from all over the world, but the region has other industries and resources besides the tourist business. International trade is very important, because the Caribbean has to import many of the goods that its people need.

Oil and gas contribute to the economies of Trinidad & Tobago and the Bahamas. These resources normally lie deep underground and require drilling, but sometimes there is oil on the surface. Trinidad's 114-acre (46 h) Pitch Lake contains nearly 7.7 million tons (7 million t) of black asphalt, which is exported for surfacing roads.

▲ Bauxite, a mineral containing aluminum, is mined in Jamaica. The island produces over 12,000 tons (11,000 t) of bauxite a year.

2% 5%

93%

☐ Fossil Fuel ☐ Hydroelectricity ☐ Other

▲ The ways in which electricity is generated in Jamaica.

1%

99%

☐ Fossil Fuel ☐ Other

▲ The ways in which electricity is generated in Trinidad & Tobago.

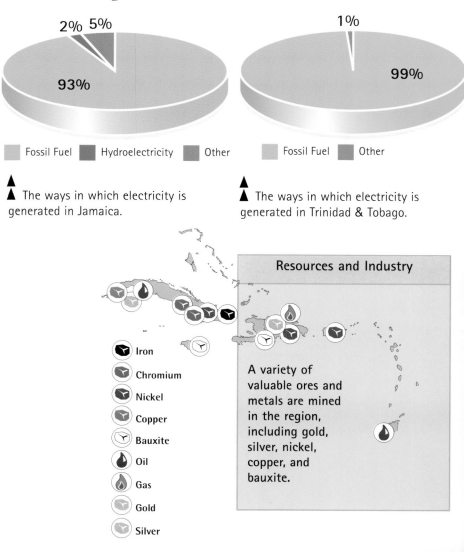

Resources and Industry

A variety of valuable ores and metals are mined in the region, including gold, silver, nickel, copper, and bauxite.

- 🜚 Iron
- ⬡ Chromium
- ⬡ Nickel
- ⬡ Copper
- 🜛 Bauxite
- 🜂 Oil
- 🜂 Gas
- 🜛 Gold
- ⬡ Silver

Tourism and other services

The Caribbean's most valuable natural resources are its tropical climate and beautiful landscapes. Sun, sea, and sandy beaches attract millions of tourists to the region every year. More than 235,000 vacationers visit St. Lucia each year. Some of the islands earn most of their income from the tourist industry.

Another important service industry is banking. Foreigners are attracted to investment in Caribbean banks because of low taxes.

Sweet trade

The sugar-making business that was developed by the colonial powers in the 16th and 17th centuries is still one of the most important industries on Caribbean islands. Sugar and rum (an alcoholic drink made from cane sugar) are mainly exported to Europe. Other industries include clothing manufacture, furniture production, and plastics.

Its warm, tropical climate makes the Caribbean a firm favorite with vacationers. Many tourists choose to island-hop on huge, luxurious cruise ships. ▼

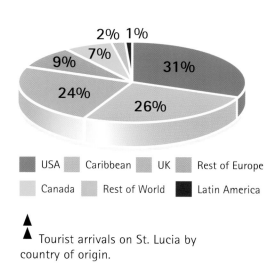

2% 1%
9% 7%
31%
24%
26%

■ USA ■ Caribbean ■ UK ■ Rest of Europe
■ Canada ■ Rest of World ■ Latin America

▲
▲ Tourist arrivals on St. Lucia by country of origin.

🌐 **Web Search** ▶▶

▶ **www.gov.tt**
Government site for Trinidad & Tobago.

▶ **www.stats.gov.lc**
Statistics from the St. Lucia government, including tourism figures.

▶ **www.caribtourism.com**
Information and links about Caribbean tourism.

Transportation

The Caribbean has a well-developed transportation system. There are good air and sea links with the rest of the world and between the islands. Roads vary in quality, but are of a high standard in the towns.

Almost all of the islands have seaports to serve tourist cruise liners, inter-island ferries, yachts, and leisure boats. Commercial harbors handle the international freight ships that bring in the goods and materials that are vital for the islands' survival.

Planes and trains

Many Caribbean islands have international airports with direct flights to and from the United States and Europe, while smaller airports offer flights between the islands.

A few of the islands have railway lines. These mostly serve the needs of sugar plantations and mines.

3% 3% 1% 1%

7%

11%

16%

30%

28%

| Container Ships | Cruise Ships | Bulk Cargo Vessels | Small Cargo Vessels |
| Passenger–Cargo | Tankers | Tugs/Barges | Car/Truck Carriers | Others |

▲ The principal types of ships visiting St. Lucia each year.

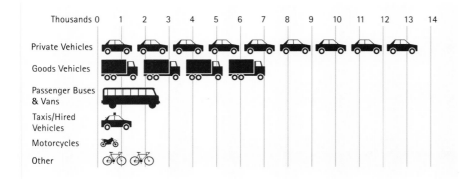

Thousands 0 1 2 3 4 5 6 7 8 9 10 11 12 13 14

Private Vehicles

Goods Vehicles

Passenger Buses & Vans

Taxis/Hired Vehicles

Motorcycles

Other

◀◀ Different types of road vehicles used on St. Lucia.

◄◄ Passengers board an island-hopper at Canefield Airport, Dominica.

Road networks

The types of roads on the islands vary widely. Those in the countryside may be little more than dirt tracks, while towns and cities have modern, paved highways.

The first roads were built to transport sugar and bananas to the ports. A network of smaller roads spread out from these freight routes. Buses and taxis operate on most of the islands today. Tourists also hire cars for getting around and sightseeing. In the countryside, donkeys and bicycles remain popular.

Road Traffic

On islands that were colonized by the French and Dutch (including the Netherlands Antilles, Guadeloupe, and the Dominican Republic), vehicles are driven on the right. On islands that were colonized by Britain (including Jamaica, Barbados, Trinidad & Tobago, and the British Virgin Islands) vehicles are driven on the left.

There are 11,622 miles (18,700 km) of road in Jamaica and over 4,970 miles (8,000 km) in Trinidad & Tobago. Barbados has just 995 miles (1,600 km) of road.

Web Search ►►

► www.mtw.gov.jm
The Jamaican Ministry of Transport and Works.

► www.stats.gov.lc/index7.htm
Vehicle statistics for St. Lucia.

► www.tradetnt.com/tt/stats/transort.html
Flight and airport information for Trinidad & Tobago.

► www.airjamaica.com
Official website of Air Jamaica.

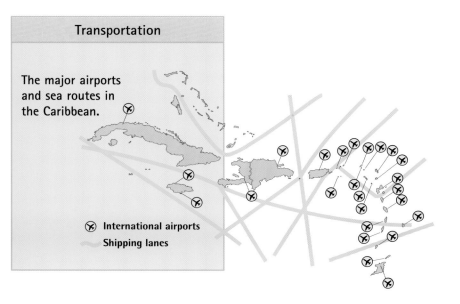

Transportation

The major airports and sea routes in the Caribbean.

✕ International airports
Shipping lanes

Education

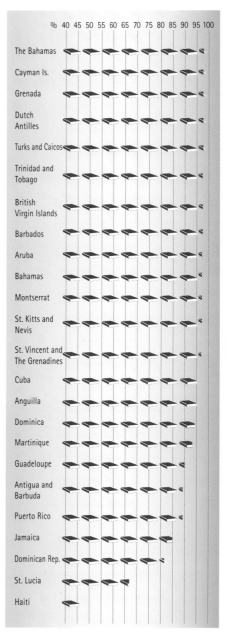

Education levels vary across the Caribbean islands. Most schools can be attended for free and are run by the government. Children study a range of subjects including modern languages, math, science, and art.

Most schools in the former British colonies are run by government education departments. The larger islands also have a small number of private schools, where families pay for their children to be educated.

On some islands, the school day starts at 7:30 a.m. and ends at 2:00 p.m. Children start attending school at about the same age as British and North American children. In Barbados, for example, children begin attending primary school at the age of four.

▲ Rates of literacy on various Caribbean islands.

◄◄ A secondary-school student on Barbados looks through a microscope during a science lesson. Science is a compulsory part of the curriculum.

18

Pupils at a primary school on St. Lucia. It is usual for Caribbean children to wear school uniforms.

Secondary school

When children are 11 years old, they start secondary school. Barbados has 22 state secondary schools, and most are coeducational—boys and girls study together. At the age of 16, students take the Caribbean Examination Council (CXC) exams. Students who stay on at school after the age of 16 take Advanced Level exams at the age of 18. Then, if their examination results are good enough, they can choose to carry on their studies at a university, college, or medical school.

Beyond school

The largest university in the region is the University of the West Indies. It has three main campuses (groups of university buildings) in Jamaica, Barbados, and Trinidad, as well as smaller branches on other islands, offering first-year courses in a limited range of subjects.

On many islands, adults who have trouble reading and writing can attend adult literacy classes at night schools.

Web Search ►►

► **www.moec.gov.jm**
The Jamaican Ministry of Education and Culture.

► **www.uwimona.edu.jm**
Website of the University of West Indies Mona campus.

► **www.ncu.edu.jm**
Website of the Northern Caribbean University.

Sports and Leisure

Caribbean athletes excel at the highest levels in international sports and track and field. The West Indies cricket team is world-famous, but other teams, including Jamaica's netball (similar to basketball) team, are also becoming well-known.

Tourists who visit the Caribbean enjoy the many sports and leisure activities that are available throughout the region. The water sports include diving, snorkeling, windsurfing, powerboating, parasailing, and swimming. Inland, people enjoy hiking, rock-climbing, and horseback-riding. Caribbean people enjoy these leisure activities, too. They also play other sports including soccer, netball, and their favorite, cricket.

Test Cricket

International cricket matches are known as test matches. They are played between the best cricket teams in the world. In the 10 years after 1976, the West Indies cricket team was almost unbeatable. It won all but two of the test matches it played.

Horse-racing at Bridgetown, Barbados. ▼

 Young boys practice cricket. Here, a boy sets up his position in front of the wicket before getting ready to play. The wicket-keeper stands in the background.

DATABASE

Famous Caribbean cricketers (and their places of birth) include:
- Curtly Ambrose (Antigua)
- Desmond Haynes (Barbados)
- Michael Holding (Jamaica)
- Alvin Kallicharran (Guyana)
- Brian Lara (Trinidad)
- Clive Lloyd (Guyana)
- Sir Vivian Richards (Antigua)
- Sir Garfield Sobers (Barbados)

Famous Caribbean track and field athletes (and their places of birth) include:
- Donovan Bailey (Jamaica)
- Merlene Ottey (Jamaica)

Web Search

► www.jis.gov.jm/sports.html
The Jamaican Information Service's sports page.

► www.westindies.cricinfo.com
Information about cricket in the West Indies.

Winter sports

Caribbean athletes compete in many of the world's events, but the Caribbean climate makes it impossible to find the right conditions to practice for winter sports. Even so, a Jamaican bobsled team has competed in three Winter Olympic Games. In 1994, at the Winter Olympics held at Lillehammer, Norway, the Jamaican four-man bobsled team came in 14th, ahead of Japan—a remarkable finish.

Daily Life and Religion

Daily life in Caribbean cities is busy and noisy. In rural areas, fewer amenities (such as roads and running water) make life quieter but less comfortable. For many Caribbean people, religion is an important aspect of everyday life.

Daily life in the Caribbean varies from island to island and between the city and the countryside. Some countries are more developed and wealthy, while others are poorer and more rural. In most places the day begins with children going to school and adults going to work in the city or on the land. Families come together again after work and school to eat, rest, and play.

DATABASE

There are good medical services in most Caribbean countries.

Infant mortality varies widely. On the most developed islands such as Barbados and the Bahamas, the rate is around 8 to 10 per 1,000 live births. On the poorest islands, such as Haiti and the Dominican Republic, the rate is 100 per 1,000 live births.

◄◄ As elsewhere in the world, shopping is a popular pastime. These people are enjoying a colorful market in St. George's, the Grenadian capital.

22

Colonial religions

Most Caribbean people are Christian. Islands that were colonized by Roman Catholic Spain and France are still mostly Roman Catholic today. Islands colonized by Protestant Britain, such as Jamaica, Barbados, and Trinidad & Tobago, are mainly Protestant. As a result of immigration from India, 24 percent of Trinidadians are Hindu, and six percent are Muslim.

Voodoo and Rastafarianism

More than half of the population of Haiti practice voodoo, which mixes Roman Catholic and African beliefs.

Rastafarianism is another popular religion, practiced especially in Jamaica. Rastafarians, or Rastas, believe that they belong to one of the lost tribes of Israel and worship the Hebrew God, whom they call Jah. They believe that one day they will return to their promised land in Ethiopia. There are about 100,000 Rastas in Jamaica.

At parish churches across Jamaica, such as this one at Mandeville, Protestants congregate each Sunday to worship. ▼

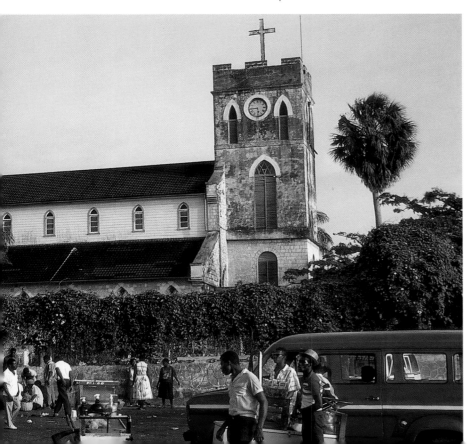

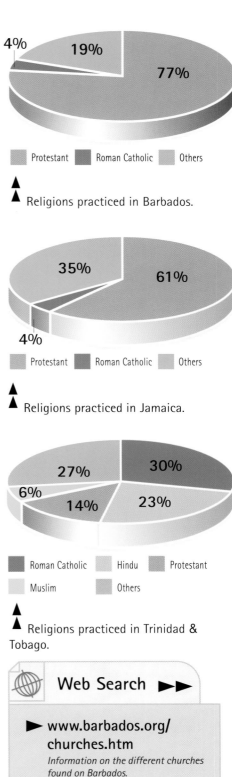

4% 19% 77%

Protestant   Roman Catholic   Others

▲ Religions practiced in Barbados.

35% 61% 4%

Protestant   Roman Catholic   Others

▲ Religions practiced in Jamaica.

30% 27% 6% 14% 23%

Roman Catholic   Hindu   Protestant
Muslim   Others

▲ Religions practiced in Trinidad & Tobago.

Web Search ►►

► www.barbados.org/churches.htm
Information on the different churches found on Barbados.

► www.moh.gov.jm
The Jamaican Ministry of Health.

23

Arts and Media

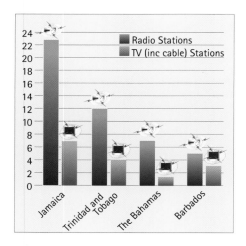

 The numbers of radio and television stations on some of the main Caribbean islands.

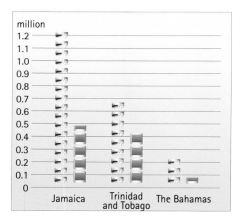

 The numbers of people owning televisions and radios on some of the main Caribbean islands.

▶▶ At carnival time on Martinique, people dress up in colorful costumes and dance through the streets.

Home of reggae, calypso, and the steel band, the Caribbean has a culture centered around music and dance. The region also boasts a strong literary tradition that has won acclaim throughout the world.

Caribbean music today can trace its roots back to rhythms, melodies, and stories brought from Africa by slaves. One type of song, called calypso, originated in Trinidad. It started in the 19th century, with slave songs about unpopular people or unhappy experiences.

Trinidad was also the birthplace, in the 1930s, of a unique musical instrument—the steel drum. It is made from the end of an oil-drum that has been hammered into a shallow dish shape and divided into areas like a tortoise's shell. The size and shape of each area determines what sound it makes when hit by a rubber-tipped drumstick.

Carnivals held all over the Caribbean buzz with the energy, color, and heartbeat of Caribbean music, dance, and costume. Carnival dates vary, but most take place around February and March, and again in July and August.

Musicians, dressed in typical colorful Caribbean shirts, play on steel drums.

Newspapers and broadcasting

Most Caribbean people enjoy freedom of speech and a free press. Many of the islands have their own newspapers, such as Jamaica's Daily Gleaner and Jamaica Observer. Other Caribbean newspapers include the Trinidad Express, the Bahamian Nassau Guardian and Barbados' Daily Nation.

Most islands have privately-owned radio and television stations, but Jamaica also has a state-run agency, the Jamaican Broadcasting Commission. Some commercial broadcasters, such as Radio Jamaica and the Caribbean Broadcasting Corporation, operate several different radio and television stations. Cable and satellite broadcasts from the United States can also be received in the Caribbean.

Famous Caribbean Authors and Poets

Trinidad-born V.S. Naipaul (1932-) has set several novels in the Caribbean, including *A House for Mr. Biswas*, *The Mimic Men*, and *Guerrillas*.

St. Lucia's Derek Walcott (1930-) won the Nobel Prize for Literature in 1992. His poetry and plays explore his mixed-race background and the Caribbean's colonial history.

Samuel Selvon (1923-94) wrote about the lives and experiences of Indian immigrants to the Caribbean.

Andrew Salkey (1928-95) was raised in Jamaica and wrote plays, novels, and poetry about Jamaican culture.

Web Search ►►

► www.jis.gov.jm/ information/culture.htm
Information on the development of Jamaican song and dance.

► www.jamaicaobserver .com
The Jamaica Observer newspaper.

► www.guardian.co.tt
The Trinidad Guardian newspaper.

► www.thenassauguardian .com
The Nassau Guardian newspaper, from the Bahamas.

Government

The Caribbean is no longer ruled by the European nations that colonized it. Most Caribbean countries are now independently governed by their own elected representatives. However, they still keep close links with the former colonial powers.

As Caribbean countries developed their own identities and grew in confidence, they increasingly wanted to govern themselves instead of being ruled as colonies by European nations. In the 19th century, the first countries to win their independence had to fight for it.

Then, during the 20th century, colonial government became less acceptable among the peoples of the world. One by one, the Caribbean colonies of countries such as Spain, the Netherlands, and Great Britain were given their independence.

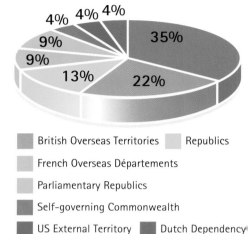

British Overseas Territories	Republics
French Overseas Départements	
Parliamentary Republics	
Self-governing Commonwealth	
US External Territory	Dutch Dependency
Parliamentary Monarchies	

▲ The percentage of different types of government in the Caribbean region.

Invasion

In 1979, a coup overthrew the government of Grenada, an independent country that was a British colony until 1974.

In 1983, a military force led by the United States invaded the island, and democracy was restored.

▶▶ The government status of different countries in the Caribbean.

Government status

Country	Status	Since	Former status
Anguilla	British overseas territory	1982	British colony
Antigua & Barbuda	Parliamentary monarchy	1981	British colony
Bahamas	Parliamentary monarchy	1973	British colony
Barbados	Parliamentary monarchy	1966	British colony
British Virgin Islands	British overseas territory	1960	British colony
Cayman Islands	British overseas territory	1962	British colony
Cuba	Republic	1898	Spanish colony
Dominica	Parliamentary republic	1978	British colony
Dominican Republic	Republic	1865	Spanish colony
Grenada	Parliamentary monarchy	1974	British colony
Guadeloupe	French overseas département	1946	French colony
Guyana	Parliamentary republic	1966	British colony
Haiti	Republic	1804	French colony
Jamaica	Parliamentary monarchy	1962	British colony
Martinique	French overseas département	1946	French colony
Montserrat	British overseas territory	1960	British colony
Netherlands Antilles	Netherlands dependency	1954	Dutch colony
Puerto Rico	Self-governing commonwealth	1952	US possession
St. Kitts & Nevis	Parliamentary monarchy	1983	British colony
St. Lucia	Parliamentary monarchy	1979	British colony
St. Vincent & the Grenadines	Parliamentary monarchy	1979	British colony
Trinidad & Tobago	Parliamentary republic	1962	British colony
Turks & Caicos Islands	British overseas territory	1972	British colony
US Virgin Islands	US external territory	1917	Danish colony

Independence from Britain

Britain granted independence to many of its Caribbean colonies in the 1960s and 1970s. They chose a variety of different forms of government. Most of them became parliamentary monarchies. Each had its own parliament, but kept the British monarch as its head of state.

Three former British colonies, Trinidad & Tobago, Guyana, and Dominica, became parliamentary republics. They are each governed by a parliament with an elected president as head of state.

Five former colonies (Anguilla, the British Virgin Islands, the Cayman Islands, Montserrat, and the Turks & Caicos) became British Dependent Territories, which are today known as British Overseas Territories. This means that as well as an elected government, they have a nominated British governor, who has some executive powers on behalf of the British government.

▲ Labor force, in millions, of some of the main Caribbean countries.

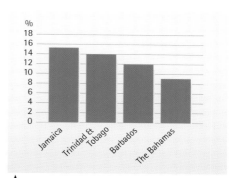

▲ Unemployment as a percentage of the total workforce.

◄◄ A soldier stands on guard outside the government offices in Nassau in the Bahamas.

Web Search ▶▶

▶ **www.gov.tt**
The official Trinidad & Tobago government website.

▶ **www.stlucia.gov.lc**
Website for the government of St. Lucia.

▶ **www.caribinfo.com/ directory/cgov.html**
The Caribbean home page for government information.

Place in the World

DATABASE

Chronology of Historical Events until the 1970s

1000
Carib Indians settle the Windward Islands

1498
Christopher Columbus reaches Trinidad

1510
Spain occupies Jamaica

1586
Sir Francis Drake visits the Cayman Islands; the Spanish arrive in Trinidad

1620s
St. Kitts becomes the first British colony in the Caribbean

1627
British colonists arrive on Barbados

1637
Sugar cane introduced to Barbados

1655
Britain takes Jamaica from Spain

1797
Britain takes Trinidad from Spain

1814
Britain takes Tobago from Spain

1834
Slavery abolished in British Caribbean

1960s
British Virgin Islands, the Caymans, and Montserrat become British Dependent Territories; Jamaica, Trinidad & Tobago, and Barbados gain independence

1968
CARIFTA is formed (see page 29)

The Caribbean lies on a major shipping route that passes through the Panama Canal, linking the Pacific and Atlantic Oceans. The different islands trade with each other and with countries all over the world. The region's natural beauty and tropical climate attract millions of visitors.

Caribbean countries belong to many of the most important international organizations, including the United Nations (UN), the World Health Organization (WHO), Interpol (the international police organization), Intelsat (an international satellite telecommunications organization), and the International Olympic Committee.

As former British Caribbean colonies became independent countries, they kept their close links with Britain. They joined a group of former British colonies from all over the world called the Commonwealth.

▼ The flags of some of the major
▼ Caribbean countries.

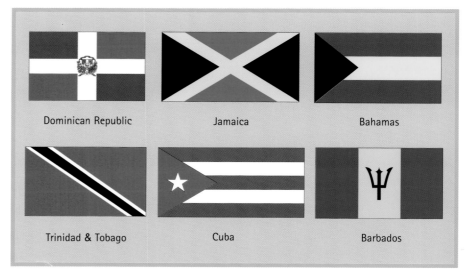

Dominican Republic · Jamaica · Bahamas

Trinidad & Tobago · Cuba · Barbados

The Palais de Justice (courthouse) at Port de France on Martinique. French Départements such as Martinique and Guadeloupe are subject to French laws and elect representatives to the French parliament in Paris.

Caribbean power

Within the Caribbean, the most important organization is CARICOM (the Caribbean Community and Common Market). CARICOM makes decisions on economics and trade that apply to all of its member countries, with the aim of benefiting the whole region. CARICOM was formed in 1973 from an earlier organization, the Caribbean Free Trade Association (CARIFTA) that was set up in 1968 by 11 former British colonies.

When the Caribbean islands were seized by European powers in the 16th and 17th centuries, most of their trade was with Europe. Now, many Caribbean countries trade mostly with a bigger, closer market, the United States.

Gross Domestic Product (GDP) for various Caribbean islands.

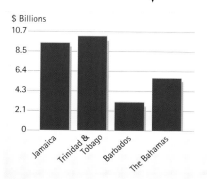

The value of yearly exports from various Caribbean islands.

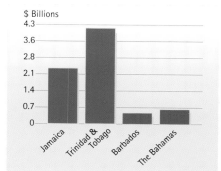

DATABASE

Chronology of Historical Events since the 1970s

1970s
Turks & Caicos islands become a British Dependent Territory; Bahamas, Grenada, Dominica, St. Lucia, and St. Vincent & the Grenadines gain independence; coup in Grenada

1981
Antigua & Barbuda gains independence; the Organization of Eastern Caribbean States forms

1982
Anguilla becomes a British Dependent Territory

1983
St. Kitts & Nevis gains independence

1995
Hurricane Luis kills at least 15 people

1997
Eruptions on Montserrat destroy Plymouth; 8,000 residents evacuated

2000
Montserrat's volcanic activity continues

Web Search ▶▶

▶ www.oecs.org
The Organization of Eastern Caribbean States.

▶ www.jftc.com
Jamaica Fair Trading Commission.

▶ www.caricom.org
Website of the Caribbean Community and Common Market.

These figures are for Jamaica, the Bahamas, Barbados, and Trinidad & Tobago.

Total Area:
11,771 square miles
(30,488 sq km)

Total Population size:
4,397,734

Capital cities:
Kingston, Jamaica
(population 538,144);
Nassau, Bahamas (172,196);
Bridgetown, Barbados (7,466);
Port-of-Spain, Trinidad &
Tobago (44,222)

Longest river:
Black River, Jamaica
(44 miles (71 km))

Highest mountain:
Blue Mountain Peak, Jamaica
(7,402 feet (2,256 m))

Jamaica's flag:
A gold saltire (diagonal cross) with two black and two green triangles. The gold represents the island's natural wealth and sunlight; the green, hope and farming resources; and the black, hardships overcome.

Official language:
English

Currencies:
Jamaican dollar (J$), Bahamian dollar (B$), Barbadian dollar (Bds$), Trinidad & Tobago dollar (TT$)

Major resources:
Bauxite, gypsum, limestone, natural gas, petroleum, asphalt, salt, timber

Major exports:
Bauxite, sugar, rum, alumina, bananas, coffee, cocoa, cement

Main public holidays:
New Year's Day (January 1)
Errol Barrow Day, Barbados
    (January 21)
Carnival, Trinidad & Tobago (mid-
    February to early March)
Spiritual Baptist Shouters'
    Liberation, Trinidad & Tobago
    (March 30)
Good Friday, Easter Monday (late
    March to late April)

Labor Day, Barbados (May 1)
Labor Day, Jamaica (May 23)
Indian Arrival Day, Trinidad &
    Tobago (May 30)
Labor Day, Bahamas (First Friday
    in June)
Labor Day, Trinidad & Tobago
    (June 19)
Independence Day, Bahamas
    (July 10)
Kadooment Day, Barbados
    (First Monday in August)
Independence Day, Jamaica
    (First Monday in August)
Independence Day, Trinidad &
    Tobago (August 31)
Discovery Day/Columbus Day,
    Bahamas (October 12)
National Heroes' Day, Jamaica
    (October 16)
Independence Day, Barbados
    (November 30)
Christmas Day (December 25)

Religions:
Protestantism, Roman
Catholicism, Hinduism, Islam

Glossary

AGRICULTURE
Farming.

ARCHIPELAGO
A group of islands.

BIRTH RATE
The number of live babies born to every 1,000 people in a year.

CLIMATE
The range of weather in a particular place over time.

CURRICULUM
A program of study.

EXPORTS
Goods sold to a foreign country.

FOSSIL FUEL
A carbon-rich substance burned to release energy, such as coal, oil, or gas.

GOVERNMENT
The organization that makes the laws and rules that apply to a country.

GROSS DOMESTIC PRODUCT (GDP)
The value of all the goods and services produced by a country in a year.

HURRICANE
A powerful storm, also called a tropical cyclone, that often occurs in the Caribbean; hurricane-force winds blow at more than 99 mph (160 kph).

HYDROELECTRICITY
Electricity generated by using flowing water to drive turbines, which turn electricity generators.

IMPORTS
Goods bought from a foreign country.

INFANT MORTALITY RATE
The number of babies who die before the age of one, per 1,000 live births.

LIFE EXPECTANCY
The average age when people die.

LITERACY
A person's ability to read and write.

MONARCHY
A form of government with a king or queen as head of state, though often ruled by an elected government.

NEW WORLD
The western hemisphere, including North, Central, and South America and the Caribbean.

PARLIAMENT
A group of people elected to represent the population in a country's decision-making establishment.

RELIGION
Belief in, and worship of, a god or gods.

REPUBLIC
A form of government, usually led by a president, in which the people or their elected representatives hold power.

RESOURCES
The raw materials, land, and people's skills that create a country's wealth.

RURAL
Describing the countryside.

SUBSISTENCE FARMING
Growing crops and keeping animals that are eaten mainly by the farmer's family, leaving little or no surplus to be sold.

TROPICAL
The part of the Earth that lies between the Tropic of Cancer and the Tropic of Capricorn; "tropical" can also mean hot and humid because of the weather conditions in the tropics.

URBAN
Describing towns and cities.

Index

Anguilla 6, 9, 18, 26, 27, 29
Antigua & Barbuda 18, 21, 26, 29
Arawak and Carib Indians 8, 9, 28
Aruba 9, 18

Bahamas 4, 6, 9, 10, 11, 13, 14,
    18, 24, 26, 27, 29, 30
bananas 11, 12, 13, 17, 30
Barbados 4, 7, 9, 10, 11, 17, 18,
    19, 20, 21, 23, 24, 26, 27,
    28, 30
British Virgin Islands 7, 9, 17, 18,
    26, 27, 28

CARICOM 13, 29
CARIFTA 28, 29
carnivals 24
Cayman Islands 12, 18, 26, 27, 28
climate 6, 7, 12, 15, 28
colonies 4, 9, 10, 15, 17, 18, 23,
    26, 27, 28, 29
crops 12
Cuba 4, 10, 18, 26, 28
currency 30

Dominica 9, 17, 18, 26, 27, 29
Dominican Republic 4, 10, 17, 18,
    26, 28

education and schools 18, 19, 22
electricity 14
employment 11
exports 12, 14, 15, 29, 30

farming 11, 12

fish and fishing 12, 13
French Antilles 4

government 26, 27
Greater Antilles 4
Grenada 13, 18, 22, 26, 29
Guadeloupe 4, 17, 18, 26, 29
Guyana 4, 21, 26, 27

Haiti 4, 10, 11, 18, 23, 26
health care 22, 23
hurricanes 6, 12, 29

imports 12, 13, 14
independence 27, 28, 29, 30

Jamaica 4, 7, 9, 10, 11, 13, 14, 17,
    18, 19, 21, 23, 24, 25, 26, 27,
    28, 30

land use 7, 11, 12
languages 9
Lesser Antilles 4, 8

Martinique 4, 18, 24, 26, 29
mining 16
Montserrat 9, 18, 26, 27, 28, 29
music 24, 25

Nassau 10, 25, 27, 30
natural resources 14, 15, 16
Netherlands (Dutch) Antilles 9,
    17, 18, 26
newspapers 25

population 8, 9, 10, 30
Puerto Rico 4, 18, 26

radio and television 24, 25
rainfall 6, 7
religions 23, 30
rural life 10, 11, 17, 22

St. Kitts & Nevis 9, 18, 26, 28, 29
St. Lucia 4, 6, 9, 10, 12, 13, 15,
    16, 17, 18, 19, 26, 27, 29
St. Vincent & the Grenadines 6,
    12, 18, 26, 29
slavery 8, 9, 24, 28
Spain 8, 9, 11, 23, 26, 28
sports 20, 21
sugar, sugar cane 8, 12, 15, 16,
    17, 28, 30

tourism 10, 14, 15, 17, 20
transportation 16, 17
Trinidad & Tobago 4, 6, 9, 10, 11,
    14, 15, 17, 18, 19, 21, 23, 24,
    25, 26, 27, 28, 30
Turks & Caicos 9, 12, 18, 26, 27,
    29

urban life 10, 11, 17, 22
US Virgin Islands 26

volcanoes 6, 29

wildlife 6
Windward and Leeward Islands 4,
    6, 28